It might be scarier . . .

At some point during the flight Tripper woke up with a start. She had just had one of her "film dreams." It went like this:

— Tripper asleep on airplane.

— Shadow passes slowly across her face.

— Camera tilts up to curtains in the aisle behind her.

— The curtains open slowly.

— In the darkness between the curtains are two yellow eyes. . . .

Tripper found herself rearranging the sequence of her dream.

"It might be scarier," she told herself, "to have the curtains opening slowly first, then the yellow eyes, then the shadow passing over my face. . . ."

Tripper tried arranging the sequence another way . . .

. . . and another way.

TRIPPER & SAM

The Phantom Film Crew

TRIPPER & SAM

The Phantom Film Crew
Nancy K. Robinson

AN
APPLE®
PAPERBACK

SCHOLASTIC INC.
New York Toronto London Auckland Sydney

ISBN 0-590-33593-6

12 11 10 9 8 7 6 5 4 3 2 1   8   6 7 8 9/8 0 1/9

Printed in the U.S.A.   06

To Rick Waddell,
who makes work fun

Special Acknowledgment

This book could not have been written without the expertise of Gene De Fever, David Eisendrath, and Richard Waddell.

PROLOGUE

Sam was Tripper's oldest friend. She had known him since she was a little girl. They had met one summer afternoon in Central Park.

It was a story they had both heard many times. . . .

Tripper's father, a documentary film director, had been shooting a film at the model boat lake. Every day a boy with reddish-gold curls showed up on his bicycle to watch the filming.

One afternoon Tripper arrived with her grandmother. She was clutching a small boat made of popsicle sticks.

"Whatever you do," her grandmother warned her, "don't fall in the lake."

Tripper took one look at her grandmother, ran to the deep end of the lake, and fell in.

Before anyone realized what had happened, the boy dropped his bicycle and ran to the spot where Tripper had disappeared. He lay down at the edge, reached in, and pulled Tripper out. He almost fell in himself.

Tripper lay on the ground soaking wet. Her eyes were closed. She wasn't moving. The boy began pressing his hand on her stomach —

". . . the way I've seem them do on those rescue shows on tv," he explained to a newspaper reporter later on. Water came out of Tripper's mouth.

"Are you breathing?" the boy asked her.

"No!" Tripper screamed and she began to cry.

The young hero was named Sam. Sam did not want a reward for saving Tripper's life. He just wanted to be allowed to hang around the film crew after school. He wanted to learn how movies were made. . . .

Going Home

Tripper left her boarding school in Colorado right after her last class. She flew to Cheboygan, Michigan, to spend the first three weeks of her summer vacation with her best friend, Katy Bear.

The Bear family had a summer cottage on an island in the Northern Woods.

On Friday, July 14th, she flew to New York and took a taxi to her father's film office, which was in a townhouse on East 50th Street and Beekman Place.

It was six o'clock in the evening in New York City and raining lightly.

Eva was sitting in the editing room talking on the phone. Eva was a film editor. She worked for Tripper's father. When she saw Tripper standing in the doorway, she smiled and waved.

"Tripper's here!" she said. "She just

walked in. I'm putting her on the nine o'clock flight. Can you pick her up at the airport?"

"Where am I going?" Tripper whispered, but Eva just handed her the phone.

"Hurry up!" Sam sounded very far away. "You're keeping everyone waiting."

Tripper laughed. Sam was in high school now. Ever since the day he had fished Tripper out of the lake in Central Park, he had worked in the film office after school. During vacations he went along on location with Roger Tripper's film crew as assistant sound man.

"You won't forget the package, will you?" Sam asked anxiously.

"What package?" Tripper asked. Just then she noticed an envelope on the table addressed to Sam. It was in his mother's handwriting and marked: URGENT! DO NOT FORGET! VERY IMPORTANT!

"I see it," Tripper said.

"Listen," Sam said. "Hold it in your hand right now, so you won't forget to pack it."

Tripper sighed and reached for the envelope.

"I'm holding it in my hand, Sam," she said.

4

"Good." Sam sounded relieved. There was a pause. Then he said, "Ready for a round?"

"Sure," Tripper said. She closed her eyes so she could concentrate.

" 'I could dance with you 'til the cows come home,' " Sam said slowly.

" 'On the other hand,' " Tripper said right away, " 'I'd rather dance with the cows until you come home!' Groucho Marx playing Rufus T. Firefly. Movie: *Duck Soup*. Studio: Paramount. Release Date: 1933. I get twenty points!"

It was a game Tripper and Sam had played for years. They called the game Next Line. It always had to be a line from a famous motion picture. If the other person got the next line right, the actor and the character who said it, the name of the movie, the studio, and the date, that person got twenty points — the highest score.

"Nope," Sam said. "The next line is, 'Yes.' Vera says, 'Yes,' and *then* Groucho says, 'On the other hand, I'd rather dance with the cows. . . .' "

"Sam!" Tripper said. "I'm going to kill you. That's not fair!"

But, at the same time, Tripper knew it *was* fair. Sam was just playing very strictly by the rules. She hadn't guessed the very next line.

Sam laughed. "Life's not fair, Tripper. You get a zero."

"I'll get you back for this," Tripper said.

"Ready any time you are." Sam was pleased. He enjoyed a challenge. "Look," he said, "I've gotta run. Your father's standing right here. He wants to talk to you."

"Hi, Dad," Tripper said.

"Tripper!" Her father sounded very happy to hear her voice. "We can sure use you around here. Everyone misses you — Nick, Coco, Carlos. . . ."

"Tell them I miss them, too," Tripper said.

Over the years her father's film crew had become her real family. They were the only family Tripper had. Her mother had been killed when Tripper was only three years old.

Nell Tripper had been a photojournalist on assignment in Honduras when her car hit a land mine. She had been killed instantly. Tripper's first name was Nell, too, but she never used it. "Just Tripper," she told anyone who asked. But she always wore her mother's ring — a strange cluster of opals and sapphires that had been given to her mother by the government of Thailand.

"I can't wait to see you," her father went on. "It's very hot and humid, but I think you're going to love it down here."

"Where are you?" Tripper asked.

Her father seemed surprised at the question. "In a phone booth, of course," he said, "outside the restaurant."

"But — "

"You won't forget your camera, will you?" he asked. "I want you to get some production stills."

Tripper sighed. "Don't worry, Dad. I won't forget."

Tripper often took photographs of her father's film crew at work. She was considered quite a good photographer, but she only liked to photograph in black and white. All that interested her was light and shadow and the different shades of gray.

"I've really missed you. . . ." Suddenly Roger Tripper sounded very busy. "Well, everyone's waiting. Wait a minute. I'd better talk to Eva."

Tripper handed Eva the phone. Eva was

winding through a roll of film. "Well, I'm looking at it right now," she heard Eva say, "and it's boring." Eva paused and listened. "Yes, Roger." She sighed. "I know it's the longest bridge in the world . . . yes, I can imagine that renting a helicopter and that special camera mount was very expensive, but the footage is still boring. . . ."

Tripper grinned. She was sure Eva was the only person in the world who could talk to her father that way.

Tripper ran upstairs to the apartment on the top floor of the townhouse and changed into her safari jacket and khaki shorts. She slipped her passport into her pocket. She had no idea where she was going. She might be leaving the country.

She dumped everything out of her soft leather traveling bag and began to repack.

Tripper could pack for any trip in five minutes. She didn't even have to think. She began stuffing her best summer clothes into the bag. Tripper had shopped for clothes all over the world and only chose fabrics that would not wrinkle. She stuck in a tin of extra dark cocoa. Tripper always traveled with her own special cocoa that came from Holland.

Carefully she placed the envelope for Sam on top and zipped up the bag.

Tripper went to the closet and got her camera case. She checked to make sure everything was there: camera lenses, filters, tripod, and darkroom supplies. She threw in a roll of wide silver tape called gaffer tape. Gaffer tape was very strong. Tripper found it came in handy for all sorts of things.

She went to the kitchen, opened the refrigerator, and took out a few rolls of film for her camera. Their refrigerator was always loaded with film. Film kept better when it was cold. There was no room for food in their refrigerator, and Tripper was feeling a little hungry.

The phone buzzed in the kitchen. It was Eva calling from downstairs.

"I'm running out to get you some Chinese food," Eva said. "How does this sound: spring rolls, two-colored shrimp, chicken with snow peas. . . ?"

"Sounds delicious," Tripper said.

And it was. Tripper sat in the editing room and ate her Chinese dinner. Eva worked on the editing machine matching sound to picture. Tripper heard a familiar voice on the sound track.

"Speed!"

Tripper sat up straight. "That was Sam's voice!" she said in amazement. "Sam said 'Speed'!"

"Speed" meant the tape recorder was now running at the right speed and ready to record. But only the chief sound man said "Speed."

"Where's Gene?" Tripper asked.

"He's working on the West Coast this summer," Eva explained. "Sam is chief sound man on this job."

Tripper was shocked. "But Sam's only in high school!"

Eva shrugged. "He's good. He's very, very good. Your father thinks Sam is going to be the best sound man in the business."

It was dark in the editing room except for the flicker of light coming from the editing machine. Tripper curled up in the big leather chair.

Tripper was tall and thin. She had very long legs, but she could curl up anyplace and make herself comfortable. She gazed at the rows of film cans that lined the walls and listened to the screeches and garbles on the sound track as Eva ran it backwards and forwards.

To many people the sound of the human

voice going backwards is very irritating, but to Tripper it was soothing. It always made her feel sleepy. She yawned.

"I think the editing room is the coziest room in the house," she told Eva.

Eva laughed. "Remember when you were a baby and we kept your playpen in here? You hated it. You shook the bars and yelled your head off."

"I don't really remember," Tripper said.

Eva worked as she talked. "Well, finally we gave up. We took you out of the playpen and let you crawl all over the place. Of course we had to put the film barrel *in* the playpen. We couldn't have you chewing up the film."

The sound track made a series of noises that sounded like "awkety gawk gawk" and Tripper felt her head begin to nod. She blinked down at her mother's ring. Just then the light caught a brilliant flash of fiery red in one of the bluish opals. Her eyes began to blur. . . .

Later on, Tripper couldn't even remember how Eva had gotten her to the nine o'clock flight that left from LaGuardia Airport.

A young man wearing mirror sunglasses

strode into the economy section of the plane. He looked around. He was pleased to see that the economy seats looked crowded together and uncomfortable. Satisfied, he returned to his seat in the first-class section.

Lance always traveled first class. He figured he belonged with what he called "quality-type people."

He was glad he was getting out of New York. Another day there and he would lose his suntan. He glanced across the aisle at the young girl fast asleep and completely relaxed. She looked like the type who did a lot of traveling. He wondered how she had gotten hold of an authentic Thai princess ring. In some parts of the world it was considered a great treasure, but Lance had no interest in opals.

Just then his eye caught the glint of something else. . . .

Night Flight

Tripper woke up and gazed out at the wing of the airplane as it flew through the night.

She found herself wishing that real life could be more like a film. In a film there are often big jumps in time. In the first shot, the audience would see Tripper's plane taking off. In the very next shot, they would see Sam meeting Tripper at the airport. Just by stringing two pieces of film together, Tripper could travel around the world in a few seconds.

Tripper watched the stewardess making her way down the aisle. The stewardess was checking to see if any of the passengers needed anything. She stopped at each seat.

It was boring to watch her, so Tripper looked around for an interesting *cut-away*.

A cut-away was another film trick to make time seem to go faster.

All at once Tripper saw the perfect cut-away.

Right across the aisle from her was a man wearing mirror sunglasses. He was tapping his ring finger on the arm of the seat.

He seemed very tense. He seemed to be waiting for something to happen.

Tripper began working what she saw into a little film sequence:

— Stewardess coming down aisle. Stops at each seat.

"May I get you anything?" she asks one of the passengers.

— CUT TO man's hand wearing ring tapping on arm of seat.

— Back to stewardess, but now she is only a few feet away.

— CLOSE-UP of man's ring tapping. Suddenly he clutches the arm of his seat. His knuckles are white. He looks as if he is about to pounce. . . .

Tripper held her breath. For a moment she was sure the man was going to leap up, grab the stewardess, and hijack the airplane.

"May I get you anything?" the steward-ess asked the man. The man just looked straight ahead. As soon as the stewardess disappeared through the curtains into the next section, Tripper saw the man relax. He looked across the aisle and saw Tripper staring at him. Tripper suddenly felt very embarrassed. Her imagination had run away with her.

The man grinned at her. He seemed to have lots of very white teeth.

"So what's happening, beautiful?" he asked.

Tripper never knew what to say when people said, "What's happening?" She wasn't even sure it was a question, so she said, "I'm fine, thanks," and looked away.

She decided she'd better load her camera before she forgot. She unbuckled her seat belt and stood up to get her camera case down from the overhead rack.

As she was loading her camera, the man leaned across the aisle. "It so happens I'm a photographer myself," he told her, "but I'm a professional. The name is Lance Dickens. I'm in the movie business. Flew in from the coast last night."

"Really? What coast was that?" Tripper

asked in her most polite voice, even though she knew perfectly well he meant the coast of California.

"The coast! The coast!" he said impatiently. "I'm a D.P. You probably don't know what that means. You see, in the movie business a D.P. is — "

"Oh, you're a cameraman," Tripper said.

Lance seemed slightly annoyed that Tripper already knew that D.P. meant Director of Photography or Chief Cameraman. He was quiet.

Lance was wearing a black silk shirt opened at the neck. He had on lots of gold chains. Tripper had never seen a cameraman who dressed that way before.

Tripper finished loading the film in her camera. As she stood up to put the case back, Lance jumped to his feet.

"Hey, let me do that for you. . . ."

Suddenly there was a ripping sound. Lance grabbed the seat of his white suede pants and sat down in a hurry. A blush began creeping up his neck.

Tripper knew he had split the seat of his pants. She reached into her camera bag and took out the roll of silver gaffer tape.

"Look," she said to Lance. "This stuff is

great for mending suede. Just tear off a piece and stick it on the inside of the seam. It won't even show."

Lance looked at the roll of tape.

"What's that?" he asked.

Tripper was surprised to meet a cameraman who didn't know what gaffer tape was.

"It's gaffer tape, of course," she said.

"Oh yeah," Lance said. "I forgot."

He grabbed the roll of tape and slid out of his seat. Tripper tried not to laugh as Lance backed through the curtains clutching the seat of his pants.

Five minutes later he returned from the rest room.

"Great stuff," he said, as he flipped the roll of gaffer tape onto Tripper's lap. She took down her camera case again and decided to make sure she had brought all the right filters for her camera lenses.

"Hi," said a little girl who was sitting in the seat next to Tripper. "I'll bet that man is happy his underpants aren't showing anymore."

The little girl spoke in a clear and precise voice. Tripper heard Lance groan.

She looked down at the little girl, who was wearing a light blue and gray candy-striped cotton knit dress. The girl had dark red hair — long and shiny — which was pulled back with two butterfly barrettes. She was wearing a large gold locket around her neck.

Tripper admired the locket.

"It's my mother's," the little girl explained. "She said I could wear it until we landed." She pointed to the woman fast asleep next to her by the window. "That's my mother," she said.

The little girl leaned forward and looked at the filter Tripper was holding up to the light. It was a dark green filter.

"That's pretty," the little girl said. "What's it for?"

"Well, actually this filter is not only for my camera," Tripper told her. "I also use it when I'm developing negatives. The negatives have to be developed in the dark, but sometimes I want to see how they're coming up. I might want to keep them in the chemicals a little longer. So I put this green filter over my flashlight and the light won't hurt the negatives."

"I see," the little girl said solemnly. "It's a beautiful green."

"It's emerald green," said Lance from across the aisle. He seemed just as interested in Tripper's collection of filters as the little girl.

Tripper handed the little girl a yellow filter. The little girl held it carefully up to the light. "What's this one for?" she asked.

"Don't let her play with that!" Lance suddenly burst out. "She might break it!"

Tripper ignored Lance. She always thought it rude when grown-ups interrupted children. "This one is called a K-2 filter," she explained to the little girl. "If you take a picture of the sky, the clouds stand out better."

The overhead lights in the airplane were dimmed. Many people were already sleeping.

"Want to share my blanket?" the little girl asked. Tripper looked down at the woolly red blanket that was wrapped around the little girl. It looked hand-knitted and very soft. Tripper was feeling a little cold.

"I would love to share your blanket," Tripper said with a smile. "That's very nice of you."

The little girl tucked part of her blanket around Tripper very carefully with her small hands.

"Okay?" the little girl asked anxiously.

"Lovely," Tripper said. "Thank you."

"My name is Amy. What's yours?"

"Tripper," Tripper whispered.

"Hi, Flipper," Amy whispered back. She snuggled up against Tripper and went to sleep.

At some point during the flight Tripper woke up with a start. She had just had one of her "film dreams." It went like this:

— Tripper asleep on airplane.

— Shadow passes slowly across her face.

— Camera tilts up to curtains in the aisle behind her.

— The curtains open slowly.

— In the darkness between the curtains are two yellow eyes. . . .

Tripper found herself re-arranging the sequence of her dream.

"It might be scarier," she told herself, "to have the curtains opening slowly first, then the yellow eyes, then the shadow passing over my face. . . ."

Tripper tried arranging the sequence another way . . .

. . . and another way.

"Wake up," a soft voice said. "We're here. We've landed."

Tripper opened her eyes and saw the stewardess bending over her. She looked around. She was the last one left on the airplane, and it was dark outside.

"You looked so comfortable," the stewardess said. "I hated to wake you." Then she laughed. "Very few people can sleep through a landing."

"I guess I can sleep through anything," Tripper admitted.

"You certainly can," the stewardess said. "Just a few minutes ago that little girl next to you was scrambling all over you. She was even crawling under your seat."

"How come?" Tripper asked.

"She lost her mother's antique gold locket," the stewardess said with a puzzled frown.

"Oh no!" Tripper said, and she thought about the little girl who had been kind enough to share her woolly red blanket.

"Well, I hope someone is meeting you at the airport," the stewardess said. "It's after midnight here."

Tripper looked out into the darkness and wondered where "here" was, but she thought it would sound a little strange to ask at this point.

* * *

Tripper walked through a room with high, arched ceilings. She found herself thinking that all airports looked alike.

She stopped short. Someone was following her.

Tripper whirled around. "Sam!" she said.

Sam was wearing his blue workshirt and jeans. He called this outfit his "filmmaker blues," and Tripper knew he only wore it when he was working. That meant her father and the film crew were out on location right now, shooting a night scene.

"Listen," Sam said. "You've got two choices. If you're tired, we can drop you off at the hotel."

"I'm not the least bit tired," Tripper said quickly.

"Good," Sam said. "We need you. Leroy is waiting outside with the van."

Tripper smiled at Sam. She thought he was looking very well. Sam had reddish-gold curls, green eyes, and a wide, thin mouth that was always turned up at the corners even when he wasn't smiling. But he was smiling now.

"All set?" he asked.

"All set," Tripper replied.

Location Unknown

Leroy was standing in front of a white film van. He was wearing a light blue seersucker suit and a white cotton shirt open at the neck.

Leroy was unit manager for Roger Tripper's film crew. One of his many jobs was to make sure everyone was on the set on time. But he never seemed to be in a hurry.

Tripper hugged him and threw her bags into the back. She climbed into the front seat and squeezed in between Leroy and Sam. Leroy turned the key in the ignition and started the motor.

Tripper put her feet up on the dashboard and leaned back. She felt right at home.

"By the way," she said to Leroy, "where are we?"

"Oh, only about forty minutes away," Leroy said cheerfully.

Sam gasped. "The package!" He turned to Tripper. "You didn't forget it, did you?"

Tripper hung over the back of the seat and unzipped her bag. She handed Sam the envelope marked URGENT from his mother.

"What is it?" she asked curiously as Sam tore it open.

"Nothing much," Sam mumbled. "Just pictures of Binker." He grabbed a flashlight out of the glove compartment and handed it to Tripper. "Hold it so I can see," he said.

Tripper shined the flashlight on the photos of Sam's dog Binker. Sam was very fond of Binker and missed him terribly whenever he went on location. Tripper had trouble understanding what Sam saw in the sluggish black dog who always seemed to be half asleep.

But, according to Sam, Binker had very complicated feelings and opinions on different subjects. He was always pointing out small changes of expression on Binker's face, but all Tripper ever saw was a look of dull, dreamy devotion to Sam.

There were pictures of Binker's birthday party, Binker at the beach, Binker watching the fireworks in Central Park. . . .

"Did your mother take them?" Tripper asked politely.

Sam nodded.

Most of the pictures were blurry and Binker's eyes often came out red. Sam's mother was an excellent librarian — she worked at the main branch of the New York Public Library — but she wasn't much of a photographer.

"What's that one?" Tripper asked.

Sam was looking at a murky bluish-black photo that didn't seem to have an image on it at all.

"Binker asleep," Sam said, and he stared happily at the print for almost a minute. He carefully tucked the photos back in the envelope. "You see, last week I had a terrible dream. I dreamt Binker was missing. So I called Mom, and —"

"Speaking of dreams. . . ." Tripper suddenly remembered the strange dream she had had on the airplane. Before she knew it, she was telling Sam about it — the curtains opening, the yellow eyes. . . .

Sam listened quietly. When she finished, he said, "And what was on the sound track?"

Tripper looked at Sam. He was perfectly serious. She thought for a moment.

"Well," she said, "now that you mention it, there *was* a sound track."

"Go ahead." Sam was a good listener.

"Let me see. Airplane motor . . . overhead blower . . . jangle . . ." Tripper began.

"Curtains don't jangle," Sam said sharply. "Where did the jangle come from?"

"I don't know," Tripper said. "It sounded like a bracelet jangling."

"Sorry," Sam said. "We'll have to leave it out. It doesn't fit."

"Hey, wait a minute," Tripper said. "There *was* a jangling sound and it was *my* dream."

Sam shrugged. "Everything can be improved," he said with a grin.

Tripper laughed. "Well, do *you* ever have film dreams?" she asked Sam.

"Of course I do," Sam said. "In fact, my dreams always have opening titles. They even have credits at the end."

They had been driving for over half

an hour when Tripper suddenly sat up straight and looked out the window. The streets had become very narrow. The buildings looked old and elegant. Many of them were surrounded by lacy wrought-iron balconies — one on top of the other. There were tiny shops lining the streets lit by flickering gaslight.

Leroy turned the corner and was forced to slow down. In front of their van was an old-fashioned buggy that was being pulled by a mule in a fancy flowered hat. The buggy had fringe on top.

Tripper had a very strange feeling. She felt as if they had driven right into the past — back into another century. The roofs stuck out at odd angles and created strange shapes. There were hidden courtyards, narrow alleyways, and shuttered windows. It seemed to be a city full of secrets.

Tripper saw a street sign that said RUE TOULOUSE. She knew *rue* meant "street" in French.

"We're getting near the old market," Leroy said. "That's where we're filming. It's a big farmers' market. Open twenty-four hours a day. Look, there's a café nearby that's always open. Why don't I drop you and Sam off? The crew is breaking for lunch."

When a film crew works at night, the midnight meal is always called lunch.

"I'll pick you up when we're ready to shoot," Leroy said.

Tripper nodded. She loved cafés. She settled back in her seat. She had figured it out. They were in a city on the south coast of France — on the Mediterranean.

The Café du Monde had green-and-white-striped awnings that hung over large arches. In front of it was a fountain lit up with colored lights. There were tables outside, but Tripper and Sam walked inside to a room with green and white striped walls, mirrors, and large fans on the ceiling.

They sat down at a table. At the next table Tripper noticed a very pretty woman dressed in a gray lace evening gown. Around her neck was the most beautiful necklace Tripper had ever seen. It was silver with droplets of bright red stones.

"They look like rubies," Tripper said to Sam.

Then she noticed the woman's companion. She poked Sam. "Sam!" she whispered.

"That woman is sitting with an alligator."

"Someone dressed as an alligator," Sam corrected her.

"Well, I realize *that*," Tripper said. "Even so, isn't it a bit *unusual*? . . ."

"You see all sorts of things here," Sam said. "Those two probably came from a costume ball. You know, today is Bastille Day."

Tripper nodded. She knew July 14th was Bastille Day in France. It was French Independence Day.

Then Tripper noticed a woman sitting at another table. The woman's face was painted white like a clown and she had large red dots on her cheeks and a huge painted red mouth. Tripper poked Sam again.

"She's a street entertainer," Sam explained in a whisper. "There are a lot of them here."

Just then a voice behind her called, "Hey, baby, what's happening?"

"Someone seems to know you," Sam said.

Tripper did not have to turn around to know who it was.

"It's Lance," Tripper whispered. "He was on my plane. I had to help him fix his pants."

"You had to help him do *what*?"

"Hey, what's happening?" Lance called again.

Tripper groaned. "What do I say to that?"

"Say, 'Nothing much,'" Sam advised her.

Tripper turned around and smiled at Lance.

"Oh, nothing much," she said.

Lance nodded and turned back to the distinguished-looking man he was sitting with.

The man had silver-gray hair and a white moustache. He was wearing horn-rimmed glasses and a turtleneck sweater. He seemed to be leafing through a script.

It was quite noisy in the café. Sam's hearing wasn't any better than Tripper's, but he was able to pick out conversations. His ears were trained to separate voices from the hum of fans, the clatter of dishes, and other noises.

"Hey, your friend Lance just asked that man what he thought of the set-up," Sam told Tripper.

"That makes sense," Tripper said. "They're probably talking about a camera set-up. Lance is a cameraman. But he calls himself a D.P., of course — Director of

Photography. The other guy must be the producer."

The waiter came over. Sam ordered a cup of café au lait, which Tripper knew was half steaming milk and half coffee.

". . . and an order of beignets, please," Sam told the waiter. "Hey, Tripper, wait until you taste these beignets." He pronounced it "ben-yay."

The waiter turned to Tripper. She was glad he understood English. It usually took her a while to remember her French.

She reached into her leather bag and took out her tin of special cocoa.

"If it's not too much trouble," she said slowly in case the waiter had trouble understanding English, "would you mind very much making me a cup of cocoa with this?"

Sam sighed and leaned back in his chair. He was used to Tripper's fussiness about getting what she called a "decent cup of cocoa."

The waiter took the tin of cocoa and looked at the label. He seemed quite impressed.

"One teaspoon of cold milk mixed with one teaspoon of cocoa," Tripper said. "Stir to a paste. Add one cup of water heated just to boiling and stir."

The waiter repeated the directions back to her. She nodded. "And we'll be happy to pay the restaurant extra for the trouble," Tripper added.

"There is no need for that," the waiter said with a smile. "We'll just charge you the price of a cup of cocoa."

"I still don't see how you can drink unsweetened cocoa without sugar," Sam said when the waiter had left.

"I like sugar," Tripper said. "I just don't like it in cocoa."

It was a good thing Tripper liked sugar. The beignets arrived piled on a plate and smothered in powdered sugar.

"There's more sugar in this shaker," the waiter told Tripper.

Beignets turned out to be square doughnuts without holes — crispy and hot on the outside and soft within.

"This is the only place they are served," Sam explained to Tripper. "It's a special recipe."

Tripper tasted a beignet and decided right then and there that she would be spending all her free time at the Café du Monde eating beignets.

"Is the cocoa all right?" the waiter asked Tripper as she took her first sip.

"It's perfect," she said. *"Merci beaucoup. Vous parlez très bien l'anglais."*

The waiter looked a bit taken aback, but he thanked Tripper and left.

Sam was staring at Tripper. "Tripper," he said, "you just told the waiter he spoke English very well."

"Well, he does," Tripper said, and she took another bite of the beignet. In the distance she heard a low, deep foghorn.

"Sounds like a big ship," she said, and sipped some more cocoa.

"It is," Sam said. "We're right on the river, even though you can't see it from here."

"Oh," Tripper said. "What river is that?" And she tried to remember if she knew any of the names of the rivers in southern France.

"The Mississippi, of course," Sam said.

Tripper almost spilled her cocoa.

"What's the Mississippi doing here?" She was almost shouting.

"New Orleans is on the Mississippi," Sam said.

A few people turned around to look at Tripper. The woman with the beautiful necklace was smiling at her. Tripper lowered her voice.

"New Orleans," she said slowly. "Do you mean New Orleans, Louisiana, U.S.A.?"

Sam was grinning at her.

"Yes," Tripper went on, almost as if she were talking to herself. "That would explain why no one asked to see my passport. I guess we *could* be in New Orleans."

"Well, of course we are," Sam said. "What did you think?"

Tripper shrugged.

"Nice place," she said, and she dipped the last piece of the delicious beignet into a mound of powdered sugar.

Night Shoot

Tripper always got a thrill when she got near the location of a night scene. The French Market was surrounded by film trucks, enormous film lights, and cables. It was only three blocks away from the Café du Monde in a large open arcade that was divided into stalls.

The first person Tripper saw was Coco, the electrician. Coco seemed to be having a good time. She was riding on the platform of a forklift. Coco signaled to the driver, and was slowly raised high enough to reach one of the big film lights hanging from the rafters. Coco adjusted the angle of the light with her heavy electrician's gloves.

"It was nice of the driver of the forklift to offer to help us," Leroy said. "You know how Coco hates to have ladders around cluttering up the set."

Tripper thought the lighting looked beautiful. There were shadows and highlights on the baskets of fruits and vegetables.

Just then she saw her father, but she knew at once that this was not a good time to say hello.

Roger Tripper was sitting behind the camera mounted on the dolly next to Nick the cameraman.

Nick saw Tripper and winked.

Carlos, the assistant cameraman, always seemed to be the busiest person on the set.

"I'd say hello," he called to Tripper, "but I'm in the bag." He had both hands in the black taffeta changing bag as he loaded film into the large film holder called a magazine.

Tripper saw John slipping a wedge under the metal dolly tracks to make them level. John was the key grip. He was in charge of all carpentry and safety on the set. Tripper was pretty sure John had seen her, but John was very shy.

Sam picked up the tape recorder and slung it by the strap over his shoulder. He put on his headphones and picked up his microphone, which was at the end of a pole called the boom. Sam called it his fish-pole and it could be extended until it became quite long. He coiled the microphone cable and held it in his hand.

Sam was going to walk behind the camera dolly as it tracked along the aisle, picking up the sounds the camera was seeing. He would be holding the boom high enough to keep it out of the shot.

Tripper knew the French Market was a difficult place to get good sound with the barkers calling out their goods: "Pecans! Pecans!" and "Step right up and get the best tomatoes in the country!"

There were other sounds, too: crates being unloaded, the rattle of the weighing scales, the man shelling peanuts. . . .

Sam would have to go back after the shot was completed and re-record many of the sounds separately. Otherwise it would just sound like a jumble of noise. A lot of the sounds he took during the shot would never be used at all.

Sam turned the knob of his tape recorder. "Testing . . . one . . . one . . . one," he called into the microphone.

Leroy met Tripper. He always jangled when he walked because he carried the keys to all the vans and storage rooms on a metal ring attached to his belt.

He grinned. "We've got quite a job for you," he said.

"I know," Tripper said. "Dad told me he wanted production stills."

Leroy shook his head. "We won't have time for that. We have something else lined up for you."

"What does Dad want me to do?" Tripper asked.

"Direct," Leroy said.

"Direct?" Tripper stared at Leroy.

"Yup." Leroy nodded. "We've already taken the shot three times tonight and it's no good. Now, as the camera moves along the aisle, we are supposed to see the vendors, the fruits, the vegetables, the spices. . . ."

Tripper nodded.

"Then, at the end of the aisle, the camera comes to rest on this kitten, who's supposed to crawl around on some barrels and sniff. The first time the camera got to the kitten, the kitten just crouched down and stared right at it."

Tripper laughed.

"On the second take," Leroy went on, "Coco said she would direct the kitten. . . ."

"And?" Tripper asked.

"Well, she did get the kitten to sniff. There was only one problem."

"What was that?" Tripper asked.

"Coco's in the shot," Leroy said. "Over the top of the barrel, you see her big brown eyes, staring at the kitten, wanting to make sure the kitten was performing properly."

Tripper burst out laughing.

"On the third take, Coco managed to stay out of the shot." Leroy sighed. "But by now the kitten is really relaxed. She's feeling like a real star. When the camera reached the kitten, she was running around and around chasing her tail."

"Well, that sounds cute," Tripper said.

Leroy shrugged. "No good," he said. "The kitten is supposed to sniff; she's not supposed to chase her tail. You see, your father wants to give a feeling of the smells of the French Market. That's a hard thing to do on film."

"So Dad wants me to direct a kitten," Tripper said.

"Well, you *are* good with animals, Tripper," Leroy said. "Remember the pig?"

Once, when they were filming on a farm in North Carolina, Tripper had to spend hours entertaining a pig. The pig was so happy to be let out of his pen, he kept digging up the grass that was supposed to look nice in the shot. Tripper had to persuade the pig not to do that.

Leroy took Tripper to the end of the aisle to meet the kitten. The kitten was an orange and white kitten — a scrawny kitten with unusually big ears. She was sitting on top of a barrel blinking at Tripper.

A lady selling eggplants at the next stand said, "Her name is Françoise."

"Bonjour, Françoise," Tripper said, and she held out her finger to the kitten.

The kitten sniffed it.

Tripper decided that the simplest way to get Françoise to sniff would be to hide behind the barrels and stick her finger up between them. She tried it.

"Looks fine," Leroy said. "Françoise is sniffing."

Tripper didn't want to overdo it and exhaust the kitten's interest in sniffing fingers, so she sat down on a barrel until they were ready to shoot.

Finally her father called out, "Stand by to roll."

A few seconds later, he called, "Roll sound."

"Speed," Sam called as soon as his tape

recorder was running at the right speed.

"Background action," Roger Tripper called.

Tripper slipped behind the barrels and began wiggling her fingers up at the kitten.

"Roll camera," her father called. "Slate it."

Tripper knew that Carlos was now standing in front of the camera with the clapperboard — a slate that looked like a small blackboard.

"Roll Fifty. Scene Nine. Take Four," Carlos called, and he clapped the boards together. Later on Eva, the film editor, would be able to match the sound of the boards clapping together to the picture of the boards clapping together.

Tripper held her breath. She knew the camera was approaching her and the kitten. But she was pretty sure the kitten was putting on a good show. She could feel the kitten's breath on her finger.

A few seconds later, Roger Tripper called, "Cut!" Then he shouted, "That was great!"

Tripper stood up and stroked the kitten. Her father came over.

"Well," he said. "You arrived just in time to save our scene."

Tripper gave her father a bear hug. Roger Tripper was shorter than Tripper. He had dark hair and bright dark eyes. He was very good-looking. And, even though he was very fussy about film, he was an easygoing father.

Sam called out, "I need a room tone."

Everyone was quiet on the set. All activity stopped.

Tripper always thought it was funny to call for a room tone outside in the open air, but she knew getting background sound was very important. There is no such thing as dead silence in the real world.

"Room tone!" Sam called.

Suddenly the sound of loud sirens filled the air. Sam sighed, turned off his tape recorder, and waited.

There were more sirens. Police cars whizzed by the French Market with their lights flashing.

Sam handed Tripper a set of headphones. He always had two extra sets of headphones — one for Roger Tripper and one for Tripper.

Tripper put on the headphones and listened as more sirens ruined the room tone.

"If we don't get a room tone soon," Sam said, "we'll be getting daytime noises.

We'll be getting the birds waking up."

"I wonder what's going on," Tripper said as two more white New Orleans Police Department cars sped by the French Market with their sirens wailing.

It took twenty minutes for things to quiet down. Sam finally got his sixty seconds of room tone.

As they were driving to the hotel, they passed the Café du Monde and saw a big police cordon around it.

Tripper was curious.

But Tripper was always curious. And, right at that moment, she was also very very sleepy. . . .

A Private Breakfast

Tripper woke up and looked around her little room. There were wooden beams on the ceiling and an antique writing desk near the window.

The film crew was staying at the oldest hotel in New Orleans. It was a very small hotel called the Hotel Maison de Ville.

Tripper was sleeping in a small four-poster bed with a gold velvet coverlet. The night before she had found a chocolate mint wrapped in tinfoil on her pillow.

"It's a tradition here," her father had told her before he kissed her good-night.

Tripper pulled back the drapes and saw Sam sitting at a table in the courtyard outside. He was wearing his khaki shorts and a loose Indian cotton shirt. His hair was wet, and every once in a while he leaned over and shook out his curls. That was the way Sam usually combed his hair.

Sam was reading a newspaper. On the table in front of him, on a silver tray, were two glasses of orange juice and a basket of croissants. Tripper watched as Sam absentmindedly picked up a long red rose that was lying on the tray. He began tapping the stem on the table, but he never took his eyes off the newspaper.

Tripper took out her camera. She crept to the window, opened it quietly, and took a picture of Sam. Sam shook out his wet hair again, and Tripper took another picture.

Sam's mouth twitched. He jerked his head up. "I saw that!" he called. He shook out the newspaper. "Just wait until you read this," he said. "You're not going to believe what happened."

"What happened?" Tripper asked, but Sam's head was buried in the newspaper again.

Tripper took a shower. She was pleased to see that there was no window in her tiny bathroom. That would make it easier to turn it into a darkroom for developing negatives.

Tripper liked to develop her negatives right on location. If she couldn't set up a darkroom, she used the black taffeta changing bag that she always kept rolled up in her camera case.

It was a hot day. Tripper put on a white cotton dress that washed like a handkerchief. It had blue flowers embroidered on the pockets. It was the coolest summer dress she had.

Under the skirts and dresses Tripper always wore old-fashioned cotton bloomers that came down to her knees. She found them comfortable and practical for taking photographs. She was always climbing and getting into funny positions.

She put her hair into a French braid and tied it with a blue ribbon. Then she slid her feet into white sandals and went out into the courtyard.

"Well," she said to Sam, "what happened?"

"Just let me finish this paragraph," Sam mumbled.

Tripper sat down across from him at the table. There was a large banana tree in the courtyard and some magnolia trees. In the middle there was a fountain with a statue of a whooping crane.

A young man brought Tripper her breakfast. On the silver tray was a pot of cocoa, a basket of croissants, and strawberry jam. Tripper also got a long red rose and her own newspaper.

She tore off the wrapping around the newspaper and spread it out. It was a New Orleans paper called *The Times-Picayune*. She stared at the headline: RUBY NECKLACE STOLEN FROM CAFE DU MONDE!

Tripper read the article quickly:

A necklace worth over half a million dollars was stolen from the Café du Monde early this morning. The necklace, which was made up of fourteen rubies averaging over four carats each, was set in silver and had been an engagement present to Miss Denise Walker, who was Queen of Rex at this year's Mardi Gras parade.

Sometime after one o'clock in the morning, Miss Walker noticed that something was wrong with the clasp. She took it off and slipped it into her evening bag. When she opened the bag again, the necklace was gone. In the bag was an engraved card: COMPLIMENTS OF THE ICE KING.

The Ice King is a well-known international jewel thief whose real name is Billy Smith. He was only arrested once in his career, but managed to escape from a Swiss jail by flying a glider over the border to Italy. . . .

"Sam," Tripper said. "Why does he call himself the Ice King?"

"Jewel thieves refer to precious gems as ice," Sam told her.

"Oh," Tripper said, and she read on:

> According to INTERPOL, the international agency that keeps records on criminals, Billy Smith is a master of disguise. The case is being handled by the United States Customs Service, which is working in cooperation with the New Orleans Police Department and INTERPOL.
>
> Anyone with any information. . . .

Just then Sam got a phone call.

". . . from a Mr. Binker, I believe," the waiter told him. Sam went to take the call in his room.

Tripper smiled. She was used to Sam getting long distance calls from his dog when he was on location. Naturally, Sam's mother put the calls through for Binker.

"Well," Tripper said when Sam came out into the courtyard again. "What did he say?"

" 'Egotist,' " Sam said, and sat down. "He said the guy was a complete egotist."

"Binker said, 'Egotist'?" Tripper asked.

"Of course not," Sam said. "My father said that. Dad's been interested in the Ice

King for years. He says he's a classic type — high opinion of self, no concern for others. . . ."

Sam's father was a professor of criminology at John Jay College in New York. Tripper liked Sam's father very much.

"What else did he say?" she asked.

"Well," Sam said, "he said that, even though the public tends to look at jewel heists as big, daring adventures, the Ice King is a dangerous type. He's perfectly capable of murder if things don't go his way."

Tripper put some strawberry jam on a croissant and took a bite. Suddenly she was aware of the whirring sound of a motor behind her. She felt a tingling at the base of her neck. She turned sharply around and looked into the lens of a movie camera that was shooting her from behind a gate.

"Sam," Tripper said. "We're being filmed."

"I know." Sam didn't even look up. He was reading the article about the Ice King over again. "It's your friend Lance. His crew is shooting a scene at the Court of Two Sisters — the restaurant on the other side of that wall."

"He has no right to film us without our

permission!" Tripper said indignantly. "We're eating breakfast. It's an invasion of privacy."

Sam looked up. "Tripper," he said gently. "If you'll remember, only a few minutes ago, while I was quietly drinking my orange juice, you were happily snapping pictures of me."

"Well, it's all right between friends," Tripper said.

Sam leaned back and smiled nicely for the camera, but, at the same time, he was muttering between his teeth: "He's a terrible cameraman. Look at him, zooming in and out, panning back and forth. He never holds the camera still. Amateurs do better than that."

"Nice. Nice," Lance called. "Looking good. Just getting some local color."

The camera motor was still going.

"I'm going to do something terrible," Tripper told Sam. "I can't help it. I feel it coming."

Tripper turned around, looked right into the camera, crossed her eyes, and stuck out her tongue.

Lance stopped filming. "Hey!" he said in a hurt voice. "What did you do that for?"

"You'll have to excuse her," Sam said. He stood up and walked over to the gate. "She has a slight nervous twitch. By the way," he said casually, "what kind of film are you making?"

"Oh, it's a big feature," Lance said. "Very big. I'm not supposed to talk about it."

Tripper joined Sam at the gate. The film producer they had seen with Lance the night before called him over.

Tripper and Sam watched as they rehearsed a scene between a boy and girl who were sitting at a table by a wishing well. In the scene the boy and girl were supposed to be having a lovers' quarrel. It ended with the girl throwing a glass of water in the boy's face.

"What a mess," Sam said. "Look at the cables all over the place. Sound cables running alongside electrical cables. I'm surprised they don't get a hum on the sound track."

Tripper was critical, too. "I don't understand the lighting," she said. "They're shooting almost at high noon and they don't even have a fill light. They'll get harsh shadows."

"I see a nice shadow," Sam said. "The

boom is casting a shadow right across the girl's face!"

They watched as Lance filmed the argument between the boy and the girl. At one point he stopped the camera and moved around the table to get a close-up of the girl throwing the glass of water in the boy's face.

"Oh no!" Sam groaned. "Lance moved too far around. The camera just *crossed the line!*"

Sam was talking about an imaginary line that all cameramen knew about. And a camera is never supposed to cross that line.

"In the first shot you'll see her yelling at him and looking to the right. Then you'll see her throw the water to the left!" Sam said.

"It's going to look pretty weird on the screen," Tripper agreed.

When the film crew was ready to take the boy's reaction shot, the assistant cameraman held up the clapperboard.

"Roll thirty-two," he grumbled. "Scene eight. Take one."

Then he clapped it together.

Suddenly he yowled and began to dance

around the patio with his thumb in his mouth.

Sam gasped. "He caught his thumb in the clapperboard!"

Tripper and Sam got a severe case of the giggles. They were laughing so hard, they had to sit down.

Shopping with Coco

Right after breakfast, Coco called Tripper's room and invited her to go shopping.

Coco loved to shop, and Tripper enjoyed shopping with Coco.

Coco always asked a lot of questions. For instance, if she was looking for a woolen scarf, she would want to know about the sheep who contributed their wool to that scarf. What kind of sheep were they? Where did they live? Then she would want to know about the dyes that were used in the scarf.

Salespeople usually enjoyed Coco. They found her lively and charming.

"Today we buy hats," Coco said as she and Tripper walked along Royal Street. "New Orleans is a wonderful place for hats. Besides, we need hats to protect us from this sun."

54

They stopped at a store called Fleur de Paris, and tried on floppy hats covered with ribbons, feathers, and lace. The woman who designed the hats was working in a room in the back. Naturally Coco had a number of questions about the hats and how the woman got her ideas for them.

Coco bought a flouncy mauve-pink hat with a bouquet of flowers on it, and Tripper picked a straw hat with a dark blue band.

They wandered in and out of antique shops, boutiques, and a shop that sold only crystal balls. The part of New Orleans they were staying in was called the French Quarter, and Tripper had never seen so many wonderful shops in her life.

When they passed The Witchcraft Shop, Coco said she was sure she needed something in there.

"I would like to buy . . . let me see." Coco looked around. "A love potion," she told the woman behind the counter. The woman had wiry gray hair. She looked like a witch.

"Yes," Coco went on, "a nice love potion I can dab behind my ears."

"But dearie," the woman said. "You must *drink* a love potion."

"Well, maybe I'd better think it over," Coco said quickly, and she hurried Tripper out the door.

They walked over to Jackson Square and walked through an alley called Pirates Alley.

"I love the names around here," Tripper said.

Jackson Square was full of people, street entertainers, and artists. Tripper saw Sam watching a man playing musical glasses.

"I'm going to have my picture painted in my new hat," Coco told Tripper, and she went to shop around for the perfect artist to do her portrait.

Tripper went over to where Sam was standing and stayed for a while, listening to the man playing songs on the musical glasses.

"It's actually a very ancient instrument," Sam whispered.

There were rows and rows of glasses on a little table. They were each filled with a different amount of water. The man played notes by wetting his finger and rubbing it around the rims of different glasses. The music was beautiful and strange. It echoed through Jackson Square.

Tripper looked around. She saw a little

girl sitting stiffly on a chair under a yellow umbrella, posing for an artist.

"I know her!" Tripper said. "I know that little girl. She shared her blanket with me on the plane coming down here."

Sam turned to look. "Oh you mean Amy?"

"How do you know her?" Tripper asked Sam.

"Your father wants her to be in the film," Sam said. "Tomorrow night we're shooting a buggy ride and your father wants a little girl sitting next to the driver. When he saw Amy sitting here, he got very excited and said she would be perfect for the buggy shot."

"Where's Dad?" Tripper asked Sam.

"Somewhere around," Sam said.

Tripper saw Leroy talking to Amy's mother. She went over to say hello.

"I'm trying to talk her into letting her daughter be in the film," Leroy told Tripper.

Tripper looked at Amy. Amy looked very cute. She was wearing a purple top and a white pinafore with ice cream sundaes painted on it. She was trying to hold very still, but when she saw Tripper, her eyes darted briefly to one side.

Amy's mother sighed. "I'm sure it would be fun for Amy," she said, "but I'm afraid it's impossible. It would be past her bedtime. Amy cannot stay up past eight o'clock. You see, we're staying with my mother down here, and she's very strict about children's bedtimes."

"Roger will be disappointed," Leroy said, "but I suppose rules are rules."

"Especially Grandmother Frances's rules," Amy's mother said with a laugh. "But does it have to be done at night?"

"I'm afraid so," Leroy said. "It's in the script. It's part of a sequence of night scenes for the end of the movie."

Tripper remembered something. She turned to Amy's mother. "Did you ever find your gold locket?" she asked. "The one you lost on the plane?"

Amy's mother looked sad. "No," she said. "It's very strange. And that locket meant so much to me."

She turned to Leroy, who was listening sympathetically. "You see," she told Leroy, "it belonged to a great great aunt who died when she was only fourteen. There is even a faded picture of Aunt Laura inside the locket. I've had it since I was a little girl."

Amy was getting restless sitting still for her portrait. She kept her eyes straight ahead, but she called out of the corner of her mouth, "Flipper! Don't go away!"

When Amy's portrait was finished, she didn't even look at it. She jumped up and grabbed Tripper's hand.

"Have you seen the Puppetorium yet?" she asked Tripper.

Tripper shook her head.

"Oh, you have to. Mommy, can I take Flipper to the Puppetorium?"

Her mother laughed. "As long as I don't have to go there again. We've been in there all morning."

Amy led Tripper into a shop full of marionettes, hand puppets, and dolls. In the back was a dark theater. There were scenes behind glass of moving puppets.

"It's a story about a pirate," Amy told Tripper, "a real pirate named Jean Lafitte who lived in New Orleans. Come look at this one. This is my favorite."

But a man was blocking their view.

"Excuse us," Amy called up to him.

Tripper recognized the familiar shape.

"Dad!" she said. "I should have known I'd find you in here."

Roger Tripper was fascinated by puppets and magic shows.

"How do you two know each other?" He smiled down at Amy.

"We met on the plane," Tripper told him.

"Well," he said to Amy, "I hope you'll be able to be in our movie."

Amy shook her head sadly. "I can't," she said. "When I stay with Grandma Frances, I have to be in bed at eight, every single night."

"Do you think we could get her to change her mind — just once?" Roger Tripper asked.

"Grandma Frances likes everything just *so*," Amy explained. "She can't stand a speckle of dirt in her house and she has rules about everything. She is very strict."

Roger Tripper could look very disappointed when he wanted to.

"I could be in it in the daytime," Amy said hopefully.

"I'm afraid it has to be a night shot," Tripper's father said. "Wait a minute!" He turned to Tripper. "Maybe we could shoot it day-for-night."

For a moment Tripper thought her father was joking. Day-for-night was a way of shooting a scene during the daytime, using a dark blue filter and special lighting to make it look like a night shot. It was tricky and difficult to get a convincing night effect.

Roger Tripper was not joking. He wanted Amy for the buggy scene and that was that.

"We'll talk it over with Leroy," he said, and led them out of the Puppetorium.

"It would be pretty complicated," Leroy said, "but, of course, it could be done."

"Sounds like fun," Coco said. "I guess we will have to shoot late in the afternoon when the sun is low. We'll need low angle back lighting or cross lighting to make it look like night."

"Late afternoon is certainly better than early morning as far as the sound track goes," Sam added. "We don't want early morning sounds."

"Let me see," Roger Tripper said. "We'll need a street that's running north. The sun should be in the west. John will have to build a high platform on the buggy so we can shoot down on Amy and the driver. . . ."

He smiled down at Amy. "Tell me, what

kind of questions would you ask the driver of the buggy? What, for instance, would you want to know about the mule?"

Amy thought a minute. "Well, I'd like to know where the mule lived, I guess."

Tripper's father laughed. "That's a good start." He turned to Amy's mother. "What about late tomorrow afternoon?"

"Sounds fine," she said. "Sounds exciting."

"Well," Roger Tripper said to Amy, "back to the Puppetorium."

Reflections on Glass

Sam asked Tripper if she wanted to go
eat some lunch. Tripper was looking wist-
fully across the street at the Café du
Monde.

"Do you think we could have some beignets first?" she asked. "As a sort of appe-
tizer?"

Sam shrugged. "It's okay with me."

So they had beignets and then went to
the Acme Oyster House. They each had a
dozen oysters, and Tripper thought they
were the best she had ever eaten.

"Now for some shrimp creole. It's a
gumbo," Sam said, and he took her to a
very old restaurant called The Gumbo
Shop. The shrimp gumbo was delicious.
"Next we go have dessert," Sam said.

"More beignets," Tripper said happily.

"Nope," Sam said. "We have to have dessert at D.H. Holmes. It's the oldest department store in New Orleans. There's a restaurant there called Potpourri and they have this fantastic sundae called a goldbrick sundae."

D.H. Holmes was on Canal Street, a wide, busy street full of traffic and shoppers right at the edge of the French Quarter.

"That's the St. Charles Streetcar. It's one of the last streetcars left in the United States," Sam said.

Tripper watched as the green and red streetcar rounded the corner onto Canal Street. It clanged its bell.

Tripper reached into her camera bag and took a picture of the streetcar, which got its power from overhead wires.

When they came to D.H. Holmes Department Store, Tripper stopped to look at a big display in the window.

It was a special display called Jewels of Mardi Gras. In one window were the Jewels of Rex — a crown and scepter that were worn each year by the King of Rex who led the big Mardi Gras parade.

"I want to try to photograph this display," Tripper said to Sam.

Sam nodded. "I'll wait inside for a table."

The display was well-lit, but the window glass caught a lot of reflections. Tripper enjoyed problems in photography. She decided to use her polarizing filter, which cut down on reflections on glass.

Tripper put the filter over the lens and twisted it around to see if she could cut down the reflections. But there was another reflection coming from the front windshield of a car parked behind her. It bounced off the window glass. The polarizing filter couldn't help cut that down.

Tripper heard a jangling noise behind her and all at once the glint was gone. Someone was standing behind her blocking it. Tripper took a picture.

"What do you want to take a picture of that junk for?"

Tripper turned around and saw Lance. He was wearing an electric blue shirt.

"Those Jewels of Rex are just paste," Lance went on. "Just costume jewelry. They're not real."

"I'm interested in photographing all kinds of jewelry," Tripper said.

"That's not jewelry," Lance said. "That's junk."

Tripper said coldly, "I'm sure that 'junk' means quite a lot to the people of New Orleans."

Lance was quiet for a moment, and watched Tripper photograph.

"Wouldn't you rather take pictures of real stuff?" Lance asked her. "Did you read about the ruby necklace? Some job, eh?"

"Yes," Tripper said. "That was terrible."

"What?" Lance seemed surprised. "What's so terrible? Anyone who can afford a necklace like that deserves to have it stolen."

"No one deserves to have anything stolen," Tripper said crossly. "Stealing is a crime."

"Oh, come on," Lance said. "A master jewel thief is no ordinary criminal. He's way above ordinary thieves. He's an artist. He's an *aristocrat* of crime. The public loves to see someone like the Ice King get away with something like this. The public looks up to him as a hero!"

"Well, I happen to be the public, too," Tripper said, "and *I* certainly don't look up to the Ice King. He's just a sneak."

Lance looked thoughtful for a moment. "Maybe the newspapers didn't do him justice. Now that I think of it, the reporter forgot to mention that he was a 'mastermind.' They usually call him a mastermind."

Tripper felt like saying, "Oh honestly!" but she kept quiet. She was relieved when Lance changed the subject.

"Tell me something," he said. "You seem to know a lot about photography: What is the best way to photograph something like a necklace? A real necklace. A necklace with precious stones."

"You mean in black-and-white?" Tripper asked. "I only photograph in black-and-white."

"Yeah," Lance said, "like for a newspaper."

Tripper was far more interested in discussing photography than the philosophy of crime with Lance.

"Well," she said, "I guess I would photograph it in daylight — under natural light."

Lance seemed quite interested, so Tripper went on: "I would set up the necklace and the camera inside a jewelry tent. . . ."

"What's that?" Lance asked.

"Well, a jewelry tent is just a piece of white cotton organdy. It's very transparent. It softens the light. It's the best way to bring out the natural brilliance of the stones."

"You certainly do know your stuff," Lance said. He seemed very impressed.

"Now, if it's a diamond necklace," Tripper went on, "it's best to photograph it on black velvet, but if the stones are colored stones — emeralds or rubies — they should be displayed on a lighter background — gray or beige. . . ."

Lance was quiet for a few minutes. He seemed to be considering something.

"Um . . . listen," he said. "I'm working on a résumé — you know, a job résumé. I'm making a list of all my successes. . . ."

Tripper found it hard to believe that Lance had had many successes as a cameraman, but she listened as politely as she could.

"I really need a good photograph of myself to send around," he went on, "something like a publicity photo. I'd pay you whatever you want if you would take a really good photo of me."

"You wouldn't have to pay me," Tripper said. "I only take photographs that interest me."

"You mean you'll do it?" Lance asked eagerly.

"Not today," Tripper said. "I'm busy, but maybe tomorrow morning."

"Do what tomorrow morning?" Sam was standing behind her, staring at Lance.

"Hey, man, what's happening?" Lance asked Sam, but he didn't wait for an answer. "I'll call your hotel tomorrow morning."

Sam turned to Tripper. "We have an early call tomorrow. At six o'clock in the morning we have to be down at the docks. Then in the afternoon we have to set up for that day-for-night shot with Amy at the corner of Chartres and Barracks Streets."

"Oh, I don't think I want to get up that early," Tripper said. "I think I'll just hang around the hotel in the morning and do some developing. I told Lance I'd take his picture for his job résumé. Oh, by the way," she said to Lance, "I can't take your picture in those mirror sunglasses."

"Don't worry," Lance said. "I'll take them off for the picture. Listen, I'm really grateful for this. And, in case you're both interested, we're shooting a really big scene tonight outside a hotel on Bourbon Street. You won't be able to miss it. We're using cameras on cranes, big lights. . . . Why don't you two drop by? You'll really see some movie-making."

"We'll see," Sam said.

"I'll call your hotel tomorrow morning," Lance said to Tripper. "Hold on a minute! I don't even know your name. What *is* your name anyway?"

"It's — " Tripper began.

"Hortense," Sam said smoothly.

"Hortense?" Lance asked.

"Yes," Sam said. "Hortense Hogg. That's Hogg with a double 'g.' "

Tripper stared at Sam. She couldn't figure out why he was saying this. Sam could keep a very straight face.

"Hortense Hogg?" Lance obviously felt quite sorry for Tripper. "It must be hard to have a name like that."

Tripper glared at Sam, but she muttered, "Yes, it *is* quite difficult."

"Well, Hortense," Lance said, "I'll talk to you tomorrow morning."

Tripper exploded as soon as Lance had disappeared around the corner. "What did you say that for?" she asked Sam. "Why did you tell him my name was Hortense Pig?"

"Hortense Hogg," Sam said quietly. "That's Hogg with a double 'g.' "

"Same difference," Tripper said.

"I don't trust that guy," Sam said. "Look, Tripper, we'll all be off shooting tomorrow morning and I don't think you should be alone with that character. He's a creep."

"We wouldn't be alone," Tripper said. "I'd take his picture in the courtyard. It's a public place. There are always people around."

Sam shrugged. "Have it your own way."

Tripper thought about her argument with Lance about the Ice King. It made her uncomfortable. Maybe Sam had been right.

"But *Hortense*," Tripper said, "of all names!"

Sam was grinning at her. "Sorry, Tripper," he said. "It was the first name that came into my head. I promise."

"You'll live to regret that, Sam," Tripper said. "Just wait."

That night Tripper and Sam went out to listen to music.

They waited on line at Preservation Hall. Jazz musicians performed there twenty-four hours a day. The concerts were held in a small room with no seats. Everyone had to stand crowded together, but Tripper thought the musicians were wonderful. It was a very exciting performance.

Then they wandered along Bourbon Street and looked in the doors of the nightclubs. In a courtyard a country music band was playing and people were dancing. Tripper and Sam went inside and danced, too. Both of them liked to dance. Then a fiddler started to play, and a friendly young couple tried to teach Tripper and Sam some Cajun dance steps.

"Someday you'll both come to Lafayette, Louisiana, and visit us," the girl said to them as they were leaving. "Then you'll hear some real Cajun music and eat some real Cajun food."

The girl gave them her address.

"Thank you," Tripper said. "That's very nice of you."

On the way back to the hotel, Tripper and Sam passed the big night scene Lance had told them about. There were crowds of people watching the filming. The hotel guests were watching from their balconies.

It was quite spectacular. Even Tripper and Sam were impressed. The cameras were mounted on big cranes and the whole area was lit up.

"Did you ever think what a wonderful cover that would be for a gang of criminals?" Sam asked.

"What do you mean?" Tripper asked.

"Well, let's say you set up this big scene and pretend to film it. Everyone is watching. Everyone is distracted. But, you see, the film crew is just a front. Meanwhile, lurking behind the scenes are cat burglars...."

"Sam," Tripper said, "I think you watch too many movies. I'm sure I've seen a movie with a plot like that."

"Are you sure?" Sam was disappointed. "I thought it was a brilliant idea. I thought I was the first person in the world to think of it."

1b...cise that HUU Ose U...Scysto
known as the Ice King, was the mastermind
behind this operation. Cards were found in
...ass every ...cunt before ...eyle...

The Phantom Film Crew

As it happened, Sam was *not* the first person to think of using a film crew as a front for a crime.

Tripper sat in the courtyard the next morning and stared at the large headlines in *The Times-Picayune*.

BIGGEST HOTEL ROBBERY
IN HISTORY.
FILM CREW DISAPPEARS.
ICE KING STRIKES AGAIN!

As hundreds of hotel guests and bystanders watched what appeared to be the filming of a high-budget feature film, the Ice King was at work behind the scenes.

Right after midnight, the film crew suddenly abandoned their cameras and equipment and disappeared into the shadows of the French Quarter. Hundreds of guests returned to their rooms to find all their jewelry and valuables gone.

It is clear that Billy Smith, otherwise known as the Ice King, was the mastermind behind this operation. Cards were found in almost every room: COMPLIMENTS OF THE ICE KING.

Tripper read the next paragraph. "They didn't even pay for the rental of the camera equipment!" she said. To someone with Tripper's background, this was especially shocking.

She went back and stared at the word *mastermind*. What was it about that word? Where had she just heard it?

Then it came to her. Lance had used it. *Well, that should make Lance happy*, she thought.

At the end of the article, it said:

Although jewel thieves do not usually carry guns, the Ice King is considered extremely dangerous, with quick and violent mood changes. The worldwide search for him has been hampered by his ability to disguise himself. Descriptions of him are sketchy. His only distinctive facial characteristic are his eyes. His eyes are said to be as yellow as cats' eyes. Anyone with any information, please call the following number. . . .

"I have information," Tripper said out loud.

A small bird with a black throat was sitting on her silver breakfast tray, pecking away at her strawberry jam.

"I have information," Tripper said again. The bird cocked its head and looked at Tripper.

Suddenly Tripper wanted very much to see someone she knew. She wanted to talk to someone on her father's film crew. She wanted Sam. She wanted her family.

But they were out shooting on the docks, and Tripper figured the Mississippi River had a lot of docks. She knew where they were shooting the day-for-night scene, but they wouldn't be there until the afternoon.

What if the authorities didn't take her seriously? What if they laughed when she told them she was actually in touch with the Ice King?

All at once she made up her mind. She had important information. She would call them and they would listen.

"After all," she told herself, "I'm not exactly a *child*!"

Tripper went through the French doors into her room. There was a briefcase and a small portable typewriter on her bed.

The phone on the antique writing desk was lying off the hook. . . .

And someone was sitting at her desk.

"Well, if it isn't my favorite publicity agent," Lance said. As he turned around the gold chains around his neck jangled. "I'm all ready to have my picture taken." He took off his mirror sunglasses.

Tripper stared into the yellowest eyes she had ever seen. They were as yellow as the eyes of a cat.

"So what's happening?" the Ice King asked her.

Day-for-Nightmare

Tripper turned to run, but Lance was too quick. He jumped out of the chair and grabbed her arm. He twisted it behind her back. At the same time, he wrapped his other arm around her neck and squeezed.

"You're not going anyplace," he whispered, "and I suggest you keep quiet." He tightened his grip on her neck. "We've got a lot of work to do."

Tripper began to choke. Lance let go of the hold on her neck. He pushed her down into the small armchair by the window.

"How did you get in here?" Tripper asked. She couldn't understand it. The Hotel Maison de Ville had excellent security.

"Well, I certainly didn't go past the desk," Lance told her. He began pacing up and down in front of her chair. "Look,

Hortense," he began, "for years I have felt that the newspapers throughout the world have not been doing me justice. As the Ice King, I am probably the greatest jewel thief of all time, but somehow the public hasn't given me enough attention — enough credit for my work."

"They *did* call you a mastermind today," Tripper pointed out.

"That's nothing." Lance seemed quite depressed. "By now the Ice King should be a legend!" He leaned down and looked intensely at Tripper. His yellow eyes gleamed.

"I have decided that you are going to write a press release about me," he went on. "You know, a few pages describing the highlights of my career. We'll send them out with a few photos — a little publicity packet — to every newspaper in the country."

Tripper had never met anyone so interested in publicity in her whole life.

"There's only one problem," Lance said. "We have to have these packets in the mail this week."

"Why this week?" Tripper asked.

"I'm glad you asked that question, Hortense," Lance said. "I have the biggest stunt of my career planned for Friday morning. The city of New Orleans will go wild. As a matter of fact, you were the one who gave me the idea."

"What are you planning to do?" Tripper asked.

"It will be a big surprise," Lance said, "a really big splash. By the time the papers get the news, they will have received the photos and releases. I'll be getting decent press coverage for a change."

"Aren't you afraid," Tripper said slowly, "that, if you send your picture out, everyone will recognize you? You'll be arrested."

"By Friday at noon, I'll be out of the country," Lance said. "Don't you see, this stunt is really 'The Farewell of the Ice King.' I've reached the time of my life when I want to try something new."

"What, for instance?" Tripper was curious.

"Oh, I don't know," Lance said. "Sheepfarming. Computer-programming."

Tripper could not believe her ears.

"But first," Lance said, "I become a legend."

He opened his briefcase and dumped an enormous notebook on Tripper's lap. "I want you to read this and pick out the best material for the press release," he told her. "I picked up that nice typewriter for you to do it on. It has to look professional. I can't type and I can't spell."

Tripper opened the notebook. It was a detailed diary of every crime he had ever committed: jewel heists from museums, jewelry stores, fancy summer resorts, homes, even palaces. . . .

"You want me to read the whole thing?" Tripper asked. "It will take hours."

And it did. She wasn't finished reading until two o'clock. For a while Lance stood over her. He kept asking, "What part are you up to now?"

Tripper would tell him. Then he would nod and say, "Oh, that's a very good part."

Tripper was bored out of her mind.

Finally Lance turned on the television set and watched cartoons while Tripper finished the diaries. She skimmed the last fifty pages.

Then she sat down at the desk and scribbled out a release. When she finished, she read it to Lance. Tripper used the corniest expressions she could think of, and Lance liked those best of all.

She typed it as he stood over her. It was

called THE ICE KING: A LEGEND IN HIS OWN TIME. Lance was very pleased with it.

Tripper had Lance sit by the French doors, and she took his photo. Tripper could not take a bad photo. Once she started, she always did the best she could. Besides, she was sure these photos could be used to identify him.

She shot up half the roll. Lance went to his briefcase and opened it. "How would you like to take a photo of this next?" he asked and he tossed Tripper the ruby necklace. It landed in front of her on the floor and twinkled up at her. Tripper stared at the necklace worth over half a million dollars.

"I want a photo of that in the publicity packet, too," Lance said. "Come on. Get going."

Tripper was a little ashamed of herself, but she was very excited about getting a good picture of the ruby necklace.

She arranged a gray pillow on the floor and placed the necklace on it. Then she set up her tripod over it, and screwed her camera onto the underside of the tripod.

She used her cotton organdy nightgown as a jewelry tent to soften the sunlight, which was now coming through the French doors at an angle. She shot down through the neck of her nightgown.

It was three o'clock by the time she was finished.

"Now what?" Lance asked.

"Now I develop the negatives," Tripper told him.

Tripper went into her little bathroom and mixed up the chemicals. She turned off the light and shut the door, but then Lance wanted to come in. He didn't trust her.

Tripper didn't particularly want to be alone in the dark with Lance, so she said she would roll the film onto reels at her desk. She would use the black taffeta changing bag.

With her arms in the sleeves of the black bag, she opened the film roll and rolled it onto a reel inside the bag. Then she felt around and placed the reel into a small stainless steel dark tank, which was also inside the bag.

She pulled out the tank.

"Is it safe now?" Lance asked anxiously.

Tripper nodded and took the tank into the bathroom. With Lance watching her, she poured the chemicals into the tank and began developing negatives. Lance got bored and went out to watch more cartoons on television.

Tripper looked at the roll when she was finished and knew she had done a very good job.

She went out. "It has to wash twenty minutes," she told Lance, and she sat down to watch cartoons with the master jewel thief.

Twenty minutes later she hung the negatives to dry with clothespins on wire hangers. She put the hangers on the shower rod and went back to watch television.

Lance stood up after a while and put the ruby necklace back into his briefcase. He took out a gold locket and held it up to the light.

Suddenly Tripper felt sick to her stomach. "That's Amy's mother's locket," she said.

"Who's Amy?" Lance asked, but he wasn't really paying attention.

"How could you do such a thing? You stole that from a child."

Lance started droning on about how clever he had been to get it off Amy's neck while she slept on the airplane.

"Shut up!" Tripper suddenly burst out. "You're boring me."

Lance grabbed her arm and twisted it again. He dragged her into the bathroom.

"All right, Hortense," he hissed. "Let's see how you did." He looked around the bathroom. "I don't get it," he said. "Where are the photos?"

"I didn't print photos," Tripper told him. "I developed the negatives."

"When are you going to print the photos?" Lance asked.

"I can't print photos here." Was Lance stupid? "I don't have an enlarger. You'll have to take them to a camera store."

"Why didn't you tell me that?" Lance was furious. "You know I can't take them to a camera store!"

"Of course you can. They never even look at them," Tripper lied. "They just put them into a big machine."

"Oh really?" Lance asked.

"Yes," Tripper went on. She was thinking fast. "They make contact sheets — you know, proofs of the negatives, and then we choose the ones we want and mark them with a grease pencil. Then they make prints."

"Oh yeah?" Lance said.

"Yes," Tripper said, "and I just happen to know where there's a camera store open on Sunday."

"Where?" Lance demanded.

"At the corner of Chartres and Barracks," Tripper said.

That was where her father was filming the day-for-night buggy scene.

"Get those negatives!" Lance said. "We're going there right now."

Tripper rolled up the negatives and stuck them into the little plastic film can that came with each roll of 35mm still film. Usually she cut them down and put them in glassine envelopes, but she wanted to hurry.

She stuck the plastic can into the pocket of her khaki jacket along with a red grease pencil. She folded up the black changing bag and put it back into her camera case. Then she slung the case over her shoulder.

Lance kept a tight grip on her arm as he led her through the back gate. He didn't let go.

When they got to Chartres Street, Tripper said, "Look, you don't have to hold my arm like that. I'm not going to run away."

Lance snorted and held her arm even tighter.

"No, really," Tripper said. "I've been thinking it over, and I feel this may be very important to my career as a photographer. But I have to get a photo credit."

"Huh?" Lance asked.

"In the newspapers," Tripper explained. "You know, it should say PHOTOGRAPH BY HORTENSE HOGG."

"Oh, I see," Lance said. He seemed to relax. He was no longer holding her arm quite so tightly. If there was one thing Lance could understand, it was the desire to get credit. "I'm sure that can be arranged," he said seriously.

Tripper suddenly felt calm. Up ahead she could see the police barricades and the buggy parked at the curb. As they got closer, she could see the whole film crew scrunched onto a platform built above the buggy.

"Hey," Lance said. "I have an idea. You could get a picture of me actually pulling this big stunt on Friday — a true-to-life photo of a heist in action."

"Fantastic!" Tripper said. "As long as I get credit."

"Sure. Sure." Lance said. And with that, he let go of her arm.

Tripper counted to three. Then she sprinted down the street and ducked under the barricades. She ran as fast as she could toward the buggy.

Out of the corner of her eye, she saw Lance duck under the barricades. For some reason all she could think about was the evidence in her pocket.

"Sam!" she called, when she reached the buggy. "Catch!" And she tossed the plastic can with the negatives up to Sam.

Sam caught it and nodded.

"Roll sound!" her father shouted.

Sam suddenly turned away from Tripper and held up his hand.

"Speed," he called.

"Roll camera!" her father called.

"Giddyap!" the driver called to the mule.

Tripper stood there in horror as the buggy with her father's entire film crew took off at a fast clip down the street.

She turned to face Lance.

"That was a very naughty thing to do," Lance said. "Now, Hortense — "

"Don't call me Hortense!" Tripper shouted as she backed away from him. She turned to run.

Wrapping Up

Tripper had run out of clever ideas. She was no longer thinking; she was running. She was running as she had never before run in her life. She knew Lance was right behind her.

She had been forced to run away from her father and the film crew — in the opposite direction along Chartres Street.

She turned right and found herself in Pirates Alley. She glanced over her shoulder and saw that Lance was gaining on her.

There weren't many people around, and Tripper couldn't figure out how to ask for help. When she turned onto Royal Street, she ran into the first shop she saw. It was a shop that sold trinkets and New Orleans T-shirts.

"Do you have a telephone?" she gasped.

The man behind the counter shook his head.

Tripper saw Lance run past the store.

She left the store and ran back down Pirates Alley toward Jackson Square. She passed a few public phones, but they were all being used.

"Excuse me," she finally said to a man using one of the phones. "I have to make an emergency call."

The man looked at her coldly. "Well, this is a business call," he said. He turned his back on Tripper and continued talking on the phone.

Tripper was stunned. But she knew she'd better not hang around waiting. If Lance caught up to her now, she was finished.

She looked around. Across Decatur Street she saw the Café du Monde. It looked so familiar. So inviting. So friendly. . . .

"The first take should be the best," Sam told Roger Tripper.

The film crew had filmed the day-for-night buggy shot three times.

"Amy sounded the most natural the first time she asked the driver those questions," Sam said. "But I'll play it back for you if you want to hear it."

Roger Tripper shook his head. "That's

not necessary," he said. "I believe you. Children get self-conscious very quickly."

The film crew was wrapping up. Amy watched them loading the equipment onto the van. She seemed to find everything the film crew did fascinating.

She followed Sam around for a while and then asked shyly, "Was I okay?"

"You were great!" Sam said. "Do you want to hear the tape played back?"

Amy nodded her head very hard.

Sam put the headphones on Amy and wound the tape back to the beginning. Amy closed her eyes and listened. Suddenly she opened her eyes wide and gasped. Then she began to giggle.

Sam smiled. People often reacted that way the first time they heard a recording of their own voices.

But Amy was giggling so hard, she had to take the headphones off. Sam turned off the tape recorder and waited.

When Amy finally stopped giggling, she just stood there gazing up at Sam in admiration. Her eyes were shining.

"Well," she said, "how did you do that? How did you get the mule to talk?"

"What?" Sam asked.

Amy sighed. "I didn't even know it was

going to be a cartoon," she said. "Animals always talk in cartoons, don't they?"

"Um . . . Amy. . . ." Sam looked at her. He was wondering if, perhaps, she was an over-imaginative child. "What did you hear the mule say?"

"Well," Amy began, "I say to the driver, 'What do you call your mule?' and then you can hear the mule saying, 'Don't call me Hortense,' and then the driver says, 'Her name is Gwendolyn.'" Amy was thrilled. "But I don't understand how you did it!" she said to Sam.

Amy expected movies to be magic, especially after all the tricks she'd seen the film crew use that afternoon.

"*Hortense?*" Sam said. "I think I'd better listen to that."

Sam put on the headphones and played the tape again. It was not unusual for a sound man to miss something in the background when he was concentrating on listening for dialogue.

Sam heard what he had missed at the time — Tripper shouting in the distance, "Don't call me Hortense!"

Sam reached into his pocket and took out the plastic film can Tripper had thrown to him.

He opened it and held the developed negatives up to the light.

"What's that?" Roger Tripper asked him. "What are you looking at?"

"Tripper's in trouble," Sam said flatly. "We've got to find her."

Sugar

Tripper was sitting at a table near the window of the Café du Monde.

Lance was across the street. He was standing in the middle of Jackson Square turning slowly around in a circle. He was scanning the area.

Tripper looked at herself in the mirror on the wall. Her eyes seemed enormous. She reached into the pocket of her khaki jacket and took out the red grease pencil. She had an idea.

Carefully, she drew a big red circle on one cheek, then on the other. She painted a big red line around her mouth. Then she reached for the shaker of powdered sugar on the table — the sugar that was supposed to be used on the beignets.

Tripper poured out a handful of powdered sugar and covered the rest of her face with it. She checked in the mirror. So far so good. She was beginning to look like one of the street entertainers.

But she had to do something about her clothes. Lance would recognize her khaki jacket.

She put her camera bag on the chair next to her and opened it. She pulled out her black taffeta changing bag — the bag she used for developing negatives. The arms in it gave her an idea.

She took out her scissors and cut a hole for the neck. Then she had to cut out the entire inner bag. When she was finished, she slipped the dark bag over her head, and pushed her arms through the sleeves. She had a new blouse.

Just then two women asked her if they could share her table. People often shared tables at the Café du Monde.

Tripper nodded and the two women sat down. She heard one whisper to the other, "She must be a street entertainer. Isn't New Orleans marvelous?"

The woman put a big straw hat covered with flowers on the table. "How did you ever let me buy this hat?" she asked her friend. Then she sighed. "It looked so cute sitting on that table at the Flea Market, and it *was* only a dollar. But I'm beginning to think it used to belong to one of those mules — you know, the mules who pull the buggies."

The woman laughed. She had a very high-pitched laugh.

Tripper looked out the window again. Lance was waiting for the light to change. He was coming to look for her at the Café du Monde!

Tripper peeked in the mirror again, and realized at once that her hair would give her away. She stared at the flowered hat lying on the table. She wanted it desperately.

Lance was now crossing the street.

Suddenly Tripper turned to the woman next to her, and said very quickly: "This-may-sound-a-little-weird-but-I'm-being-chased-by-a-master-jewel-thief-and-I-need-to-borrow-your-hat."

The woman stared at her. Then she burst into peals of high-pitched laughter.

"Isn't New Orleans marvelous?" she said to her friend, and she handed Tripper the flowered hat.

"Darling," she said, "you can keep it."

Tripper put on the hat.

A few seconds later, Lance walked into the Café du Monde.

He looked the place over carefully. Then he left.

Tripper knew she had to get help right away, but her legs were trembling so violently, she couldn't stand up.

A waiter came over to the table to take their order. The two women asked for café au lait and beignets. The waiter turned to Tripper. Tripper opened her mouth to say something. Then she closed it again.

Her voice wasn't working.

The two women offered to treat her to something, but Tripper just shook her head and stared down at the table. She couldn't figure out what was wrong with her. She knew the danger was over, but it was as if the terror of the day had hit her all at once.

After the women had eaten and left, Tripper remained sitting and staring down at the table.

"Are you all right?" the waiter asked.

For the first time Tripper looked up. Right behind the waiter she saw her father coming toward her. Sam was right behind him.

Her father came straight to the table, sat down, and put his arm around Tripper. Sam sat on the other side.

"I had a feeling we'd find her here," she heard Sam say.

Tripper turned to her father. "I . . . I. . . ."

"You don't have to talk now," her father assured her. "Everything's going to be all right."

Sam got up to make a phone call. When he came back, he said to Tripper's father, "He's meeting us here."

Tripper felt as if she were sitting in the midst of a dense fog. She wondered who they were waiting for. A few minutes later, Sam looked over at the door.

"That must be him," he said, and he waved.

A man in a pale yellow shirt and white pants came over to their table. Tripper looked up at him.

He was young and quite good-looking. He had dark blond hair and a moustache. When he spoke, he spoke with a soft Southern accent.

"I'm Bruce Jones," he said to Tripper. "United States Customs."

Tripper looked up into the kindest blue

eyes she had ever seen and burst into tears.

She felt the tears streaking down through the powdered sugar that was plastered all over her face.

"There's nothing to be afraid of anymore. You're in good hands," Bruce Jones said. "You'll feel all right in a few minutes," and he sat down across from her at the table.

It was then that Tripper and Sam learned that they were now under the protection of United States Customs.

Tripper felt a little better after she had drunk two glasses of milk and eaten a whole plateful of beignets.

She used a napkin dipped in a glass of water to wipe the sugar off her face.

Then the four of them took a walk along the river. They strolled along a boardwalk called the Moonwalk and talked.

"The first thing we have to do is come up with a code name for each of you," Bruce explained. "For your own safety you have to remain anonymous. In a big cooperative effort like this between ourselves, the police, and INTERPOL, you will be referred to in all communications by a code name."

Sam seemed to enjoy the idea. "Maybe my code name should be Mike," he said thoughtfully.

"Mike as in Michael?" Bruce asked.

"No," Sam said. "Mike as in microphone." Sam changed his mind almost at once. "No," he said. "I want to be called Panda."

"Why?" Tripper asked.

"I don't know," Sam said. "I just do."

"What about you?" Bruce asked Tripper. "We want you to pick a code name you'll be happy with."

"Sugar," Tripper said.

Bruce laughed. "Sugar sounds just right."

Tip-off

In many ways life went on as usual during the next week.

The film crew remained at the Hotel Maison de Ville. Tripper and Sam went out on location with them each day.

But there were always undercover agents around, keeping an eye on them — making sure they were safe.

Sam was pretty sure he could pick out the undercover agents.

"I'll bet it's those guys on the ladder fixing the sign over the pastry shop."

And when they were filming from a steamboat on the Mississippi:

"I'm sure it's that deckhand who keeps folding chairs and setting them up again."

But most of the time they just knew they were under constant watch.

A customs agent was assigned to the

telephone switchbox in the basement of the hotel. From there he could listen in on any calls Tripper received in her room in case Lance tried to contact her.

Bruce Jones did not want them seen going into the United States Customhouse, which was a few blocks away on Canal Street, so once a day he would meet them in a public place. They might walk around Jackson Square eating ice cream cones or take a ride on the St. Charles Streetcar through the Garden District.

Bruce was very easy to talk to. When they talked to Bruce, they found themselves remembering things about Lance that hadn't occurred to them at the time: Was he left-handed or right-handed? Did he have any special gestures or habits?

Sam was very good at remembering things like that. He had a way of being able to imitate people — the way they walked, the way they talked. . . . He noticed the smallest details.

Tripper's negatives had been printed by the photo lab at Customs. The prints were sent to INTERPOL in Paris, the New Orleans police, and the agents watching the train station, airports, and bus terminals.

The authorities didn't want the newspapers to publish the photos yet. They didn't want to force Lance to work too hard on a new disguise. They were sure he was still in New Orleans.

One thing kept bothering Tripper and she mentioned it over and over to Bruce.

It was the big "stunt" Lance said he was planning for Friday.

"He said I'd given him the idea, but I can't remember what I said or did," Tripper kept saying.

On Thursday afternoon the film crew filmed a scene in the Dungeon Room at Restaurant Antoine, the most famous restaurant in New Orleans. During breaks the waiters brought them samples of food to taste: barbecued shrimp, steak, oysters Rockefeller, pommes soufflés, which were large, round, crispy fried potatoes served in a basket made of woven bread and fried potatoes. Then they brought samples of desserts: chocolate mousse, meringue glacé. . . .

After the crew was finished shooting, they went to Brennan's. . . .

". . . for breakfast," Coco announced.

"Breakfast?" Tripper asked. "But it's five o'clock in the afternoon!"

"One always has breakfast at Brennan's," Coco told her.

They sat in a beautiful courtyard at glass tables surrounded by palm trees. Tripper ordered eggs sardou and Sam had crayfish in hot spicy sauce. For dessert everyone had bananas foster — flaming bananas served with vanilla ice cream.

At nine o'clock that night they all had dinner at Galatoire's. Tripper thought they served the best seafood she had ever eaten in her life.

When she got back to her room, she decided she would never eat again — not for a few weeks anyway.

But the chocolate mint was lying on her pillow, and, after all, it was her duty. . . .

At eight o'clock Friday morning, Tripper and Sam sat in the patio eating breakfast. The crew was out reshooting the helicopter sequence. They were shooting without sound, so Sam had the morning off.

There wasn't any mention of the Ice King in the newspaper. The press had been asked to play down the story.

The main news was about a hurricane hovering in the Gulf of Mexico. The National Weather Service said there was a possibility it would hit New Orleans.

The phone in Tripper's room rang and she went to answer it.

It was Bruce Jones. "Something's up," he said. "I'll be right over."

When Bruce walked into the courtyard, Tripper took one look at his face and knew Lance had pulled his "stunt."

Bruce was furious. "The Jewels of Rex are gone," he said. "They disappeared from the window of D.H. Holmes a half an hour ago. Every agency in New Orleans is on alert."

"The Jewels of Rex?" Sam stared at Bruce. "I don't believe it. That's like stealing the Mardi Gras."

Bruce nodded. His face was grim. "I just finished talking to the Chief of Police and he said his department would do everything in their power to help us recover those jewels. You see, that crown and scepter may not be worth much in terms of dollars, but they sure mean something to the people of New Orleans."

Tripper groaned. "That's exactly what I said to Lance. I *did* give him the idea."

"No, you didn't." Sam was as angry as Bruce. "He thought it up all by himself in that distorted mind of his."

The phone was ringing in Tripper's room.

"Wait a minute," Bruce said, and he went inside to the front desk of the hotel. A minute later he returned.

"They're holding the call," he said. "I'm sure it's Lance. He asked for Miss Hogg in Room 10. I want Tripper to take the call in her room. Sam, I want you to listen in at the switchboard at the desk, and I'm going down to the basement to listen in at the telephone switchbox."

"What do I say to him?" Tripper asked.

"Whatever you feel like saying," Bruce told her quietly.

Tripper went to the phone in her room. She waited to give Bruce and Sam a chance to get to their posts. Then she picked up the phone.

"Hortense." Lance was whining. "I'm very disappointed in you."

"Oh, why is that?" Tripper's heart was beating very fast.

"I still don't know why you gave those negatives to your brother."

"Oh, it was just a joke," Tripper said. So Lance thought Sam was her brother.

"I don't even know your brother's name," Lance whined.

"It's Humbert," Tripper said. "Humbert Hogg with a double 'g.' "Tripper knew Sam was listening. She couldn't help herself.

"Well, Hortense," Lance went on, "I've accomplished my mission. I have become a legend. Guess what I have in my briefcase."

Tripper knew he had the Jewels of Rex, but she pretended to guess:

"A diamond ring?"

"No." Lance was gleeful now. "Guess again."

"The Crown Jewels?" Tripper asked.

"You're getting close," Lance said modestly.

Tripper sighed. She knew she wasn't doing a very good job of guessing, but she wanted to keep Lance on the phone as long as she could.

"Is it bigger than a breadbox?" she asked.

"Huh?" Lance said. Then he shouted, "It's the Jewels of Rex. I've got the Jewels of Rex!" and he hung up.

Tripper went out to the courtyard. Sam came out a minute later. He was grinning at her. "Humbert?" he said.

"You deserve it," Tripper said.

"Other than that," Sam said, "you did a

good job." He sat down at a table in the courtyard.

Bruce came out a few minutes later. He was very discouraged.

"There's no way to trace that call," he told them. "All we know is that he called from a public phone at a busy intersection. There are a lot of busy intersections in New Orleans on a Friday morning."

Tripper looked at Sam. He was staring off into space. He seemed to be daydreaming. He put his elbows on the table and ran his fingers through his curly hair. Then he closed his eyes and leaned back in the chair.

Tripper turned to Bruce.

"Sam heard something," she said matter-of-factly. "Something important."

"How do you know?" Bruce asked.

"That's how he looks when he's trying to remember a sound he heard."

"Well, then, we'll play the conversation back to him." Bruce was very excited.

"You won't have to," Tripper said. "Sam has an excellent memory for sound."

Sam shook out his curls and stretched his arms. He yawned and opened his eyes.

"The streetcar bell," Sam said with a grin. "I heard the clanging of the streetcar bell."

Pursuit

The St. Charles Streetcar runs through the Garden District — a quiet grassy area. There is only one busy intersection on the route where the streetcar always clangs its bell and that is when it turns onto Canal Street at the edge of the French Quarter.

Lance had called from a public phone at the corner of St. Charles Avenue and Canal Street — only a few blocks from the hotel.

Bruce had to make a quick decision. "Look, I can't leave you alone here," he said. "You're coming with me, but you'll have to obey orders."

There was an unmarked Customs car waiting outside the hotel. Bruce introduced both of them to the driver, an agent named Karen McGee.

"Sit in the back seat," he told them, "and

keep your heads down. I don't want Lance to see you."

At the corner of St. Charles and Canal Streets, Bruce jumped out of the car with his hand on his gun.

Lance was already in a taxi. The taxi was pulling away.

"Look at that. He's waving to me," Bruce muttered.

Bruce called for assistance on his car radio as they swung through the streets of the French Quarter in pursuit of the taxi.

At Basin Street, Lance jumped out of the taxi and disappeared through the gates of the St. Louis cemetery.

Bruce got out of the car and went after him. Tripper and Sam stayed in the car with Karen. They stared into the strange cemetery.

The cemetery looked like a miniature city.

"In New Orleans we call these cemeteries Cities of the Dead," Karen told them. "The ground is low and wet and the Mississippi has flooded its banks many times over the centuries. People didn't want their loved ones washing away so they built the tombs above ground."

"I wouldn't want to chase someone

around in there," Tripper whispered to Sam. She was relieved when police cars began arriving and surrounded the cemetery.

Forty-five minutes went by. The search continued, but Lance was nowhere to be found.

Just then a call came in over the car radio. Somehow Lance had managed to get to Union Station. He had run onto the platform and jumped on the train just as it was pulling out. He was now on board the Southern Crescent heading for New York City. Lance was being held on the train by the conductor.

Bruce got on the radio again. "Stop the train when it slows down near the power station," he called into the radio. "We'll meet it up there."

The chase was on.

But as soon as they arrived near the power station, they learned that, once again, Lance had escaped. As soon as the train had slowed down, he had leaped off. He was now heading on foot toward Lakefront Airport — just a few hundred yards away.

Karen swung the car around and headed for the airport. Just then the radio dispatcher asked for a report on the condition of Sugar and Panda.

"Sugar and Panda: safe and sound," Bruce said, and he winked at Tripper and Sam.

They were almost at the airport when there was an update:

Lance had hijacked a plane — a hurricane hunter that belonged to the National Weather Service. It was a twin-engine propeller-driven plane used to fly into the eye of hurricanes in order to collect data. Lance was taking off alone from Lakefront Airport.

"Head for our hangar," Bruce told Karen. He turned around. "Look," he said to Tripper and Sam, "I'm a pilot and I'm going after him. We have a plane in the hangar that's faster than the one he's in. I may be able to catch up with him. Karen will take you to the control tower. You'll be all right there."

Tripper and Sam reached the control tower just in time to see a yellow plane with black and white checkered wings roar down the runway.

"That's Bruce's plane," an air traffic controller told them.

"Wow!" Sam said. He knew about airplanes. "It's a P-51, a Mustang. A World War II pursuit plane!"

"That's right," the air traffic controller said, "and one of the best planes ever made for this kind of flying."

"Where did they get one of those?" Sam asked.

"Same place they get pretty near their whole fleet — from the smugglers they catch," the air traffic controller told him. "Smugglers have very good taste in aircraft."

Tripper and Sam sat quietly and listened. All of a sudden, a call came in from Air Control One stationed off the coast of Scotland. All international flights were being affected and all air traffic in the immediate area was either grounded or redirected to other airports. No one wanted other planes getting into the middle of a chase over the Gulf of Mexico.

Tripper and Sam knew that the situation was dangerous, especially with a hurricane in the Gulf. The air is turbulent for hundreds of miles around the eye of a hurricane.

They wanted Lance to be caught, but, more than anything, they hoped Bruce would get back safely. Over the past week, they had both become quite fond of their Customs agent.

An hour later the goods news arrived:

Lance had been forced down thirty miles to the east of New Orleans on a small island.

"Strangely enough," the air traffic controller told them, "the name of that island is Diamond Island."

The Secret Friends
of Rex

"Lance is crazy," Bruce said. "He must think he's the greatest pilot in the world."

Roger Tripper was listening intently to Bruce's account of the airplane chase. "What did he do?" he asked.

"When I first saw him," Bruce said, "he was a couple of miles ahead. I ordered him to fly back to the airport. Instead he turned around and flew straight at me."

Tripper gasped.

They were sitting over dinner at a restaurant called K-Paul's. It was Bruce's favorite restaurant in the French Quarter. It wasn't fancy, but it was famous throughout the world for its spicy Cajun food.

"What did you do?" Sam asked.

"Well, I was pretty sure he wouldn't ram me," Bruce said. "I just didn't want us both to turn away in the same direction at the same time, so I kept going."

"Then what?" Sam asked.

"At the last second he pulled up," Bruce said. "As he passed above me, he shouted into the radio, 'Ooops, sorry, I missed you that time.' I think he was more interested in showing off than in getting away."

"Sounds like Lance," Tripper said.

"At one point I looked ahead and saw the darkest clouds that mark the area of the eye of the hurricane," Bruce said. "Lance was heading right toward the eye!"

"Go on! Go on!" Roger Tripper said impatiently.

"Suddenly he changed his mind. He dove into a cloud and hid. I estimated where he would come out of the cloud and went after him. I flew under him and slightly behind. Then I fired a warning burst of machine gun fire close enough to scare him. We have tracer bullets mixed in with the others so I knew he would see it."

Bruce's eyes twinkled. He leaned forward and said, "Then I got to say it!"

"Say what?" Sam asked.

"Well," Bruce said, "I got to say, *'Land as directed or I'll shoot you out of the sky!'*"

Suddenly Bruce looked down at his plate and blushed. He seemed a little embarrassed.

"I've always wanted to get a chance to say that," he mumbled.

Lance did what he was told. When Bruce took him into custody, he shrugged and said, "You win." That was all he said.

The Jewels of Rex were recovered. So were many other precious pieces of jewelry, including the ruby necklace and Amy's mother's gold locket.

"I don't think we'll be hearing from the Ice King again," Bruce said.

That night the Mayor of New Orleans announced that there would be a special parade the following Saturday to celebrate the recovery of the Jewels of Rex.

"The City of New Orleans owes a tremendous debt of gratitude to the heroic actions of two young people whose names, I am told, must remain a secret," the Mayor added.

"New Orleans loves parades," Bruce said. "And it loves secrets."

It was the night of the special parade. The entire film crew, along with Tripper and Sam, were standing on a balcony over-looking Royal Street. They were waiting for the parade to begin.

"We're not filming this one," Roger Tripper said. "For once in my life I want to watch a parade just for fun."

For some reason that made Tripper very happy.

Amy was on the balcony, too, along with her mother and her Grandma Frances. Grandma Frances would never let Amy stay up late to be in a film, but a special parade in New Orleans was an entirely different matter.

Grandma Frances smiled at Tripper. She had soft brown eyes and beautiful white hair. She was wearing a lavender voile dress with a lace collar. Just below one shoulder she wore a diamond pin in the shape of a crown.

"Grandma Frances was once Queen of Rex," Amy said proudly, "and once you are Queen of Rex, you get to wear that pin for the rest of your life."

Bruce took Tripper and Sam aside. "We've received a flood of mail," he said, "addressed to the Secret Friends of Rex — that's you two."

"What kind of mail?" Sam asked.

"Invitations from all the social clubs that put on the annual Mardi Gras parade each year. You see, they are rivals. They compete for the best costumes, the best floats, the best parties," Bruce said, "but the Jewels of Rex have always been the symbol to all of the spirit of the Mardi Gras."

"What kind of invitations did we get?" Tripper asked.

"Let me see," Bruce said. "The Krewe of Rex wants their Secret Friends to attend a masked ball at midnight; the King and Queen of Comus have invited you to be presented at a special session of their court — there is even an invitation from the Social Club of Zulu to visit their secret den. It comes from the Big Shot of Africa, one of the most popular figures at our Mardi Gras parade. That's quite an honor."

Tripper sighed and looked at Sam. "Isn't there some way we could go?" she asked Bruce.

"Only if your identities remain a secret," Bruce said, "and I don't know how we'd manage that."

Suddenly the air was filled with the sound of sirens.

Tripper felt a thrill as three police

motorcycles with red and blue flashing lights came slowly up the narrow street to lead off the parade. Next came the police mounted on horseback. . . .

"Look at the pigs!" Amy shrieked with delight.

On the first float were two enormous pigs made of papier-maché. One was named HORTENSE and the other HUMBERT. The pigs nodded and bowed to the crowds.

Bruce sighed. "As I was saying, New Orleans loves secrets — more than any city in the world. There's only one trouble: Secrets get around very fast in New Orleans."

Sam leaned over and waved to the pigs. Suddenly he turned around. "I've got an idea," he said. "We could go underground. We could become alligators."

Bruce looked thoughtfully at Sam.

Late that night, after the parade, two anonymous alligators with a police escort were given a very special tour of New Orleans.

"But we're not allowed to talk to the press," Tripper whispered to Sam.

"Alligators don't talk anyway," Sam whispered back. "Only mules talk."